BAEP

Lyra and the Adventure of the Flying Fish.

Lots of love from Lyra XX
+ rabbit

YOUNG LION
Playful and fluffy-coated, this young cub will soon grow to the sleek proportions of an
adult lion.

ART PUBLISHERS

Everybody
Any Country
Every world
Anywhere

ART PUBLISHERS (PTY) LTD · DURBAN · JOHANNESBURG · CAPE TOWN

SOUTH AFRICA

PRINTED IN SOUTH AFRICA   COPYRIGHT
IMAGES AVAILABLE FROM www.artpublishers.co.za

Lyra and the Adventure of the Flying Fish

ISBN 978-1-907912-01-6

Published in Great Britain by Phoenix Yard Books Ltd
This edition published 2011
Phoenix Yard Books
Phoenix Yard
65 King's Cross Road
London
WC1X 9LW
www.phoenixyardbooks.com

1 3 5 7 9 10 8 6 4 2
Set in Garamond Book and Aunt Mildred

Book design by Insight Design Concepts
Printed in Singapore
A CIP catalogue record for this book is available from the British Library

Lyra and the Adventure of the Flying Fish

Written by Peter Emina

Illustrated by Alice Ridley

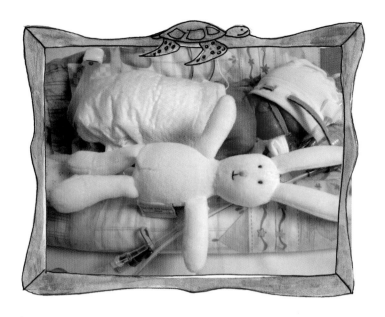

Lyra and W. Rabbit were together from the very first moment. As the second moment arrived, Rabbit lay there with his head next to hers. He could feel her tiny breaths pass along the hard plastic tube which the doctors had fitted to help Lyra's not-quite-ready lungs puff, pant and gasp. He listened to the air as it passed his big furry ears.

Lyra and the Adventure of the Flying Fish

This story is dedicated to, and inspired by, Lyra McConnell.
It's about her too. Well, sort of ...

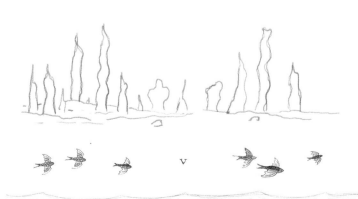

Lyra was floating in what could have been a giant bath. It was so warm and wet, but salty too. It had to be the sea.

Somewhere in her head a memory was wiggling, just out of reach. The salty, warm, wet sea reminded her of something … or maybe it was somewhere … or even someone. She couldn't quite remember.

Above her the sun shone, ignoring everything and getting on with its shining. But below her things were happening.

A fishy world raged below the shimmering, splashing surface of the sea.

Lyra floated on her tummy, peering down into the deep. W. Rabbit, his long ears twitching as the waves tickled them, floated alongside keeping her safe from the dangers below.

She floated there listening to the world becoming LOUDER and quieter as the waves slopped around her ears. She felt the hot brightness of the sun on her back and the warm, softness of the sea on her front.

At first there was only one slippery flash of silver moving so fast Lyra couldn't be sure she'd seen anything at all. But then, they were everywhere. The gently splashing sea became a heaving mass of foam and flashing silver shapes.

A hundred flying fishes burst through the surface and carried Lyra upward on a whooshing tangle of fish and foam, fizzing like an over excited ginger beer. Lyra screamed as they rocketed upwards. The flying fish stared back at her with big shiny eyes and, although their mouths opened and closed, they said nothing to the hitchhiker on their backs.

Girl, fish and rabbit flew above the waves.
Girl, fish and rabbit.
Fish and rabbit.

Lyra tumbled back into the sea and disappeared.
Fish and rabbit flew on.

For seconds that seemed like minutes the world went silent as Lyra vanished beneath the waves. By the time she bobbed back up, she was alone.

The flying fish had gone and taken W. Rabbit with them.

Lyra wasn't scared, she was terrified.

W. Rabbit was the first thing she'd ever seen. He had been there next to her for her whole life, keeping her safe from the strange and dangerous world.

Now he was gone. But the world was still there, strange and dangerous.

Now he was gone, anything could happen.

"R-A-A-A-A-A-A-A-BBBBBBBBBB-I-I-I-I-I-I-I-I-I-I-I-I-TTTTTTTTTTT!" screamed Lyra. Salty tears fell from her eyes and joined ten million, million others that had formed the sea.

"RRR-a-a-a-a-a-a-BBBBBBBBi-I-I-I-I-I-i-I-I-I-I-I-TTTTTT!" she called again, but she knew it was useless.

W. Rabbit never answered when she called.

He never replied when she spoke to him either.

He was just THERE.

Always.

But Lyra's shouting had not gone unnoticed. A large, weed-covered rock was heading slowly towards her. Lyra saw it coming out of the corner of her eye and thought, if Rabbit were here a rock would not be trying to sneak up on me.

She decided to ignore it so it would go away.

The rock was now quite close, so ignoring it took a lot of concentration, but Lyra was an expert ignoror. She floated on her back and stared up into the sky, humming to herself a little to make it quite clear to the rock that she hadn't noticed it and that it might just as well go away.

But the rock kept on coming, and by now was almost within touching distance, despite the best bit of ignoring Lyra had done for a long time.

She tried harder and flipped over onto her tummy, staring down into the water. Her humming drifted out of her mouth and up her plastic snorkel until they burst out into the air above.

"Hmmmmm-hmmm-Hmmmm-HHHHMMMM-hm".

Then Lyra stopped, very suddenly, right in the middle of her fifth hum.

She popped her head to the surface again and, forgetting her plan to ignore the rock, stared straight at it.

"Yes, that's the rock," she said to herself, and then bobbed back below the surface again and stared some more.

Up-down. Above-below. On the surface-underwater.

Lyra bobbed until she was sure.

Above the water the rock was a rock.

Below the water it had four legs and a beaky-looking face.

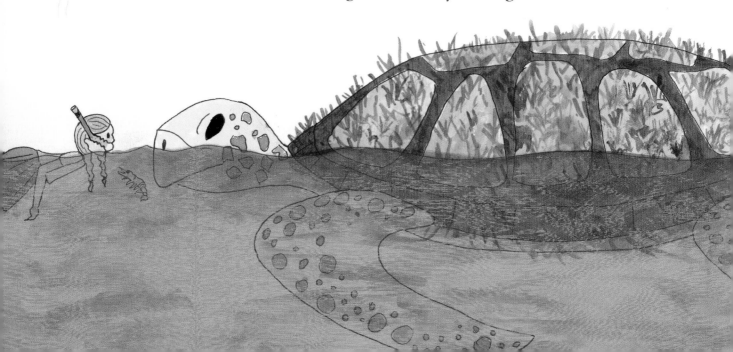

The rock was huge, many times bigger than Lyra, who was now face to beaky face with the rock.

A prawn drifted between them.

SNAP! It was gone, into the rock's beaky mouth.

"WAAAAAAAAAAHHHHH!!" Lyra screamed. The rock looked shocked.

"Oh I am most terribly, terribly sorry. How rude of me," said the rock. "I should have offered that tasty treat to you first."

That is what the rock said but, because its head was underwater, all Lyra heard was, "Buurbbledd … buuubbbleeely … blubblub … gurgleblub."

She signalled for the rock to put its head above the surface so that they could talk properly. Lyra wanted to ask if it knew where the flying fish had taken Rabbit, but she had never met a talking rock before so didn't know what to say. She decided that being polite would be her best plan.

"Good afternoon, Mr Rock," said Lyra. "I'm so glad we ran into each other like this."

The rock looked puzzled and frowned. He glanced over his shoulder. Well actually, what would have been his shoulder if he hadn't been a rock, as if he was checking that they were alone.

"A pleasure? I rather thought you were trying to ignore me."

Lyra laughed. "Why on earth would I do that, Mr Rock?"

The rock's watery eyes settled on Lyra. "Why do you keep calling me 'Mr Rock?'" he asked.

"Well, I'm sorry, but I've never met a talking rock before," replied Lyra, "and I don't know your name, so Mr Rock seemed …"

"It's Timothy," interrupted the rock, "And I'm not a rock. I'm a turtle!"

"A turtle?" repeated Lyra. She was more ready to believe in a talking rock than something called a turtle. "What's a turtle?"

"I am. I'm a turtle," replied Timothy. "On the outside turtles have a big shell that keeps us safe and we live inside, protected from the strange and dangerous world."

"Oh, I see," Lyra said. She had been feeling rather scared since W. Rabbit had gone and thought that living safe inside a big shell seemed like a very good idea. "I wish I had a big shell to live inside. W. Rabbit always kept me safe, but now the flying fish have taken him and I don't know if I'll ever see him again!" she sobbed.

Timothy thought to himself for a few moments and then suddenly his back legs, front legs and lastly his head disappeared inside his shell.

Lyra was disappointed. She'd hoped Timothy would help her find W. Rabbit, or at least have some idea where the flying fish might have taken him.

She stared at the giant shell as it bobbed up and down on the waves and, as she stared, a crack appeared in the side of the shell.

The crack got bigger until it became a door; a door with a very small creature standing in the doorway.

"Come along, come along. Get inside quickly!" called the strange creature in a squeaky shout. And, because Lyra was alone, in the middle of the sea, she thought she might as well go in.

Timothy closed the door behind Lyra and they stood staring at each other. "Are you still a turtle?" Lyra asked.

"Of course I am," replied Timothy crossly. "How could I suddenly be something else? I was a turtle when you were outside and I'm still a turtle now you're inside."

Lyra thought for a moment. She was about to ask if all turtles were like him but thought better of it and, instead, she said she was sorry if she'd upset him.

"It's quite alright. You know you are probably the first non-turtle ever to set foot inside a turtle's house."

Lyra looked around as Timothy led her across to the sofa.

Inside, Timothy's house was very grand indeed. A sparkling chandelier hung from the beautifully decorated ceiling and the walls were covered in paintings of very fine looking turtles.

Timothy sat opposite Lyra on a rather uncomfortable, but splendid looking, green chair with swirly gold legs. Lyra was on a matching sofa, equally splendid and equally uncomfortable. They drank tea without milk from tiny gold-rimmed cups.

Timothy was a very well-mannered turtle. He sat upright, his legs carefully crossed, stirring his tea in perfect circles so that every sugar crystal had an equal ride on the golden brown merry-go-round in his cup.

Lyra watched carefully as he stirred. She thought that anyone who took so much trouble being fair to sugar crystals must be someone she could rely on to help her find her lost rabbit.

Girl and turtle chatted about this and that. Timothy told Lyra how he had inherited such a magnificent house and Lyra told Timothy how she had been separated from W. Rabbit.

Finally, she asked if he would help find him.

"HOORAY!" shouted Timothy, so loudly that his squeaky voice hurt

Lyra's ears. "Hooray! This is
what I've been dreaming of.
An adventure!" Timothy bounced
around the room. He jumped on
the table, pointing at his relatives
in the paintings and laughed.
"I'll show you!" he shouted.

"Ha ha ha, Uncle Benedict! Ha ha
haaa, Great-Aunt Augusta! Haaaa haaa ha haa, Grandfather!"

Timothy would have carried on ha ha-ing when his grandfather's
painting, which did not approve of such behaviour, raised a
disapproving eyebrow.

Meanwhile, Lyra wondered whether asking for Timothy's help was such a good idea.

Timothy was standing on gold and glass table when he eventually stopped bouncing.

He looked Lyra in the eye and said excitedly, "We must leave right away. Where has your Mr Rabbit gone?"

Lyra looked back at Timothy tearfully. "I don't know where he's gone. That's why I asked for your help!"

Timothy's excitement sagged, "Oh, right, of course. Err … hmmm. So, flying fish? How were they flying?"

"What?" asked Lyra.

"I mean, were they flying in one big jumble, crashing and thrashing around, or were they a precision team, flying in neat lines, wing tip to wing tip?"

"They were all jumbly," sniffed Lyra.

"Jumbly you say? Well then, there's only one place they could be heading and Uncle Percy can help us find them. Let's go!"

Timothy jumped down from the table and strode across to the statue of Great-Uncle Percy who, until this point, was minding his own business in the corner. Great-Uncle Percy's statue was very unusual.

It was really two statues in one, each with its own Percy face looking in a different direction.

If Lyra looked at the statue from one part of the

room, Percy looked like a rather fine sea captain, with a telescope in one hand and a bit of sailing equipment in the other. But, as she moved round in another direction, he seemed to be dressed as a castaway.

"Percy was my family's greatest adventurer," said Timothy proudly. "If the artist had been able to build a statue with fifty faces that would have only just been enough for each of his adventures. He's the only turtle to have flown with the flying fish."

"Excuse me, Uncle Percy," said Timothy, grabbing hold of his great-uncle's head and turning it right around so that the captain's head was on the castaway's body. The castaway was now dressed as a captain.

As the faces finished their journey there was a very loud 'Clunk!' and the whole room shuddered.

The paintings flipped round into sea charts and maps full of twinkly lights and rows of numbers. The marble mantelpiece disappeared into its own fireplace and seconds later reappeared as a control panel. Levers, knobs, buttons and meters, all with twitching needles, lined up beneath a huge screen showing the swaying seaweed and flapping fins of the watery world outside.

Lyra watched wide-eyed as Timothy's armchair became a steering wheel.

She felt the sofa fidgeting beneath her and jumped up just in time as it transformed itself into two seats, which shuffled themselves into

position in front of the controls.

Everything was now quiet, except for an efficient-sounding hum from the control panel and a jauntier hum coming from Timothy.

Timothy had slipped on a stylish sailing outfit with white trousers and a blazer.

"Do you think I should wear the hat like this, or more like this?" asked Timothy adjusting his captain's hat to a cheeky angle.

Lyra was getting impatient and somewhat annoyed with the time it was taking for Timothy to get going.

"For goodness sake, please can we hurry up? We need to find Rabbit!"

Lyra's bad-tempered words rushed across the room and slapped a shocked Timothy across the face. He stopped adjusting his hat and bustled across to the pilot's chair, muttering to himself as he went. Then he plonked himself down, pressed half a dozen buttons in a very brisk and efficient way and suddenly they began to move.

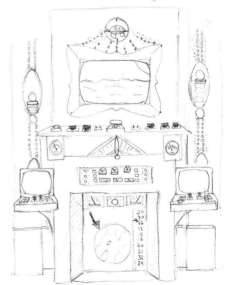

Like a rock heading off on holiday, the huge turtle splashed its way forward through the little waves that tickled its tummy as they passed by. Below the tickly waves, four giant flippers flapped the turtle-shell ship forward. Inside, Timothy stood, his hands on the wheel and his eyes on the horizon.

Lyra sat staring at the massive screen that showed them the view outside.

A view of nothing.

Well, nothing but sea and sky.

Sea and sk …

Sea and s … sea!

"We're sinking!" shouted in Lyra as the water gurgled around them. "We're sinking!"

"Calm down, dear. We're not sinking! We're diving," replied Timothy smugly.

Lyra felt a little bit silly, but it had been a very upsetting day for her so far. She covered up her embarrassment with a casual, "Oh, of course," and wandered over to look out of the huge window, which had once been a painting of Great-Aunt Augusta.

Outside, the undersea world stretched out all around them. Above, she could still see the sunlight dancing on the surface, but below it was getting darker and colder. She shivered to think that W. Rabbit might

spend forever, lying on the cold, dark seabed, waiting to be rescued by her. She tried to stop thinking about a future without him.

But how would she ever be able to find W. Rabbit?

Timothy wasn't thinking about the poor wet rabbit. He was thinking about his adventure. But where was it, this adventure? He'd had more exciting times in the bath. He wanted an adventure with sudden terrors and death-defying narrow escapes; a rescue mission steeped in danger. This was more like a stroll along the beach to get an ice cream.

Then, Timothy saw it. The scariest shadow in the sea slipped quietly over him and for an instant everything went black. Over at the window, Lyra shivered as 400 jagged razor-sharp teeth cruised by.

Brrrr, she thought.

Hmmm, thought Timothy. I wonder how much adventure I can take?

But Timothy didn't wait to answer the

question. He pushed the speed controller as far forward as it would go and headed off after the teeth.

What was that? wondered the shark, as he was hit by a speeding rock.

What on earth was going on? He was a shark after all. Everyone was scared of him.

BANG! It had happened again. The shark turned his enormous head and came face to face with a girl staring out of the window.

The shark opened its mouth, but it didn't really seem like it wanted to bite her. It looked like it was about to speak. But Lyra didn't want to know what it might say. She stared at those hundreds of teeth and screamed:

"SHHAAAAAAAAAAAAAAARRRRRRRRRRRRRRRRRRRRK!!!!!"

"Yes I know," laughed Timothy. "Isn't it exciting?" And with a flurry of lever-pushing and pulling he spun the turtle around and headed off at top speed, away from the shark who was now chasing after them.

"Woooohoooo!" whooped Timothy as they whooshed through the water, swerving around banks of coral, dodging lumps of rock, blasting through forests of seaweed. All the time the shark sped after them.

The bubbles left by the turtle's madly flapping feet burbled past the shark's face and over his gills. They tickled as they popped and made him laugh and, although a laughing shark might look happy to other sharks, all Lyra could see were those teeth. So a laughing shark seemed even scarier.

Timothy had begun to wonder if his idea of livening up his adventure by bumping into the shark had been such a good idea. He'd noticed that the shark was gaining on them and the turtle was already going at top speed.

Life and death adventures had seemed a lot more fun when he

was reading in bed and it wasn't actually his life and death having the adventure.

The turtle churned through the water as fast as it could.

And then it didn't.

The turtle shuddered, stuttered and sneezed to a stop.

Hanging in the water, between a sleeping jellyfish and some passing seaweed, Lyra and Timothy watched in horror as the shark torpedoed towards them.

He wasn't laughing any more.

"This is not quite the adventure I'd planned," said Timothy, his voice quivery. "I'm sorry. We might not find your Mr Rabbit after all."

The thought of not finding W. Rabbit scared Lyra more than the shark's 400 teeth.

If Rabbit were here he'd have kept her safe.

If he'd been here this wouldn't have happened. The strange and dangerous world with its strange and dangerous sharks would have kept away.

At that moment, Lyra decided she'd like her last thought to be about W. Rabbit. He had been there at the beginning and so she wanted him to be there at the end.

She imagined feeling his soft furry body next to her and his whiskers tickling her ear as his nose twitched and she felt happy and brave.

"Goodbye, Lyra," said Timothy, and closed his eyes.

"Goodbye, Timothy," replied Lyra, and closed hers.

"Hello, Turtle," said the shark.

Lyra and Timothy peeked out from under their hands.

"Look, I just wanted to say I'm really sorry. I kept bumping into you back there. I can be a bit clumsy sometimes. Where are you headed?"

The shark waited expectantly, pushing himself forward until his nose was pressed against Great-Aunt Augusta's window.

"You're sorry?" Lyra and Timothy finally asked together.

A stream of bubbles slipped from the shark's mouth as he sighed.

"Thank goodness for that. For a moment I thought you weren't going to accept my apology."

Timothy and Lyra looked at each other then smiled weakly at the shark.

"Super. I'm so pleased that's sorted out. Well, I'd better be off. Don't want to be late for lunch."

But Lyra was not scared of the shark anymore, since she'd thought about W. Rabbit she felt different. Lyra thought she'd ask him for his help.

"Mr Shark, would you help us please? We're trying to find someone," she said.

The shark listened carefully to Lyra's story and then asked, "How were the flying fish flying?"

"The fish were flying in a sort of big jumbly all-over-the-place whoosh!"

The shark smiled, "A jumbly whoosh you say? Well, I think we all know where they were heading, don't we?" And he nodded at Timothy, who did know, and at Lyra, who didn't.

"Why does everyone know where Rabbit is apart from me?" Lyra moaned.

"Well, it's so obvious," replied the shark, "but knowing wouldn't help you anyway, because you'd still need this turtle's help to get there as you seem to be a stranger to these waters."

Timothy fidgeted. He was still looking rather pale from his life and death adventure a few moments earlier.

"Um .. " said Timothy.
"Did you say something?" asked Lyra
'Um....um.....'" repeated Timothy.

"What are you muttering about? I can't hear a word you're saying. Timothy, Come on let's get this thing going again. We've got to rescue

W. Rabbit!" pronounced Lyra.

Realising that Timothy looked sort of pale green instead of his bright emerald colour, she added, "Timothy, are you feeling alright?"

"Er … I might need to go and lie down for a while. That adventure was a bit more adventurous than I'd thought it would be. I think I might just stay here and lead a quiet life for the next sixty years," whimpered Timothy.

"But you promised to help me! You said you wanted an adventure. You said …" cried Lyra.

"I know," Timothy replied in a very little voice, "but I've realised I don't really like adventures very much in real life. One short adventure is quite enough for me."

"Well I'm not giving up … ever! I'm going to find some way to rescue Rabbit". And although Lyra felt like crying, she knew she would have to be brave.

"Perhaps I can help," interrupted the shark. Timothy and Lyra had been so busy with each other they had forgotten all about the cause of their disagreement.

"I could take you there," continued the shark.

Lyra looked puzzled "I don't really see how. You're a shark and I'm a girl. We don't really go together."

"Well, it just came to me as I was about to head up to the surface and grab some lunch. I could take you with me. You could just hold onto my fin and we'd be up there in no time."

Lyra thought about it. Could she trust the shark? He seemed very polite, charming even. But she'd never seen so many teeth in one mouth before, and it was lunchtime.

Something hissed close to Lyra's ear. "Psssssssst."

It was Timothy trying to attract Lyra's attention.

"You can't go with him! I know he looks very friendly and all, that but he's a shark and sharks can't be trusted."

Lyra stared out the window at the shark. He was huge, his mouth was enormous and it was filled with row after row after row of sharp teeth. He was terrifying even when he was trying to look friendly. Lyra turned from the window and looked at Timothy

"Well, I don't have a choice, Timothy. I've got to risk it if I'm ever to find Rabbit. I have to say yes. I'm sure it'll be fine. Goodbye, Timothy, and thank you for your help."

Timothy didn't reply. He watched Lyra pick up her snorkel and followed her silently to the front door and watched her step out into the ocean. As the shark slipped past, Lyra grabbed the big fin on his back and in seconds they were almost out of sight. Two shadows, rocketing up towards the sunlit surface.

Timothy slowly closed the door and walked back though his empty house to the control room. He began fiddling with the back of the panel to find what had caused the breakdown and within a few seconds found a loose wire. He reconnected it and the efficient "hhhhuuummmmm" returned.

Everything was working properly now and he could head off wherever he wanted.

He could travel to that lovely warm island he had visited last week, or maybe that bay on the mainland, which had so many tasty things to eat.

But somehow those places didn't have the same appeal before. He didn't care any more about basking in the sun or eating fresh shrimps.

For some reason he couldn't quite work out, he did care about Lyra.

Even though he wasn't sure why, he knew he had to find out if Lyra

was safe, so he set off after Lyra and the shark.

Timothy crashed through the sparkling surface where the two worlds met and brought his turtle craft to a halt. Adjusting his captain's hat to a jauntier angle, he shielded his eyes from the sunlight streaming through the top hatch he'd just opened and climbed up towards the

sky. He'd followed what he thought was the same path to the surface as Lyra and the shark, but now he was here he couldn't see them. But then his eyesight was pretty bad.

Timothy carefully adjusted his monocle, raised his binoculars and scanned the ocean, searching for Lyra and the shark. At first it seemed like there was nothing. But then, Timothy's binoculars revealed a frenzy of activity.

The turtle muttered to himself, listing each new even that caught his eye: "Seagulls squabbling over sardines. A fleet of jellyfish heading off on voyages of discovery. A shark thrashing about trying to bite a small girl. A hermit crab practicing kite-surfing. A mermaid ... What?" shouted Timothy and spun his binoculars back.

"A shark trying to bite a girl! I knew he couldn't be trusted."

Timothy jumped back down into the cabin, slamming the hatch behind him and shouting orders to himself as he marched across to the control panel. He grabbed of bunch a levers, pushed some buttons and with a lurch the turtle craft started off towards Lyra and the shark.

Timothy could see them both through the screen that was the turtle's eye. Lyra was hanging on desperately as the shark lurched and bucked and twisted, as he tried to flip her off his back and into his mouth.

"She can't hold on forever," Timothy yelled to himself. "If her grip slips she'll be gone in a chomp!"

Across the waves Lyra's grip was indeed starting to weaken. She was feeling bruised and dizzy from being thrashed about, but knew she had to hold on, because the only place she was safe from 400 snapping teeth was on the shark's back.

By now the shark was very angry that Lyra was not cooperating by becoming his lunch. He thrashed more wildly, lurched more suddenly, then bucked more powerfully than ever. Lyra's grip loosened and she shot straight up into the air. As she headed up, she saw what looked like a large rock zooming across the waves towards the shark.

The whole turtle shook as it sped across the sea. Faster and faster. Timothy pressed more buttons and pulled more levers. Faster and faster, but still not fast enough.

Lyra stopped heading upwards and, after a strange moment when she just hung in mid-air, she started to fall back down towards the shark's waiting mouth.

Down, down, down she fell, and as she got closer, and closer, and closer, the shark's mouth got bigger and bigger and bigger. But Timothy was getting nearer and nearer and nearer.

It was a race between turtle, teeth and tumbling girl.

Inside the turtle, Timothy was searching frantically for an extra burst of speed. He was very close now and, even though he had no idea how he was going to rescue Lyra, at least he was almost there.

Lyra was almost there too … but she wasn't so keen to arrive.

Looking into the black hole of the shark's mouth she could see the remains of breakfast still stuck in his teeth. She didn't want to join it.

The shark licked his lips,

Timothy pressed a button,

Lyra closed her eyes and … Chomp!

The shark's mouth snapped shut.

Everything was silent, and then SPLASH!

Lyra landed in the sea next to the shark's head.

She opened her eyes and stared at the shark, who stared back at her with a shocked expression on his face and a huge rock stuck in his mouth. Suddenly, a door opened in the side of the rock and Timothy appeared.

"Quickly Lyra, get in!" he shouted.

The turtle held out a hand to pull Lyra inside before the dazed shark worked out what was going on.

Lyra threw her arms around Timothy and hugged him until his monocle popped out of his eye.

"Timothy, thank you," said Lyra "you really did save my life. That was so brave."

For the first time in his life the turtle began to feel like a hero, like his relatives in the paintings.

"GHHHUMMMMPPHHH!"

Lyra and Timothy had forgotten something.

"GGGHHHUUMMMMPPPHHHH!"

Something very important.

"GGGGGGGHHHHHHUUUUMMMMMPPPPHHHHHHH!"

They had forgotten that the turtle-shell ship was still stuck inside the shark's jaws! And he was choking.

"GGGGGGGGGGGGHHHHHHHHHHHHHUUUUUUUUUU-
MMMMMMMMMPPPPPPHHHHHHHHHHHHH!!!!!!!"

The shark heaved, gave an enormous cough and the turtle blasted from between his jaws and out across the sea. Inside the shell, Lyra and Timothy fell in a heap as they bounced across the waves like a skimming stone, leaving the spluttering shark far behind.

Eventually they stopped skimming and with a splash the turtle shell landed. Lyra and Timothy picked themselves up and staggered giddily over to some chairs and slumped down.

"Are you okay, Timothy?" asked Lyra smiling as the room spun around her.

"I think so. Are you?" the turtle gripped the side of the chair.

"Yes, thanks to you. But where are we?
Do you know?"

Timothy didn't. "I think we might be lost" he said.

Lyra stopped smiling. She had been rescued from certain death but now seemed further away than ever from Rabbit, who was the reason she had risked death in the first place.

There was silence, then a rather sad little sniff from Lyra and then, without warning, Timothy was surprised to hear himself saying, "Don't worry, Lyra. We'll keep searching until we find W. Rabbit, no matter how long it takes, no matter what dangers we have to face. We'll keep

on until we find him and he's back with you."

Timothy grabbed her hand and led her up through the top hatch into the sunshine above.

Together they stared out towards the horizon but could only see the usual ocean waves.

But then, as they watched, the gently splashing sea became a mass of hissing foam and silver shapes.

The flying fish had returned!

Hundreds of them burst through the surface. But something about these fish was different. They were not a jumbly whoosh. They were flying in straight lines. Row after perfectly spaced row circled the turtle

ship twice then dived back into the sea a short distance away.

"Well, that was a stroke of luck!" cried Timothy, "Of all places to end up. We're here!"

"Here? Where's that?" asked Lyra, sniffing a bit more.

"At the School of Flying Fish, of course! Those fish you just saw have learnt to fly in formation and soon will be going solo, but the fish that took Rabbit were all over the place and so they were probably on their way to flying school. They're probably still here being trained."

"You mean Rabbit's here?" exclaimed Lyra.

"Well let's go and see, shall we?" replied the turtle, and they both headed back down the hatch into the control room.

From inside the cabin they saw the last of the fish touch down on the flying school runway. On one side, another group of flying fish were sitting in rows listening to a lecture and there, at the end of the third row, next to a rather fat-looking fish with a big moustache, was someone who very definitely was not a flying fish.

It was W. Rabbit!

"RRAAAABBBIIITTTT!" shouted Lyra at the top of her voice through the cabin window.'

"RAABBBIIITTT!" and fifty fishy faces turned towards her.

"Oh dear." said Timothy "They look rather upset."

But they weren't.

After a second or two, the fish students all burst out laughing. Even the veteran flyer giving the lecture managed a smile before whacking his pointy stick on the complicated aeronautical diagram he was explaining on the board.

"Settle down now, chaps." shouted the lecturer. "Settle down."
He turned to face the turtle-shell ship. "Now look here, turtle. I'm afraid you can't come bursting into here like that," he continued crossly, "There are proper channels for applications to join the flying classes. Anyway this is the advanced class and you seem … well, you need … well, you are …"

But Timothy interrupted before he could finish.

"I haven't come to learn to fly, Captain Finn. I've come to fetch one of your students who's here by mistake."

"By mistake? Impossible!" bellowed the fish. "All of these students

had their names down as soon as they hatched. They all enrolled together and come from long family lines of flyers. They all …" He paused and thought for a second. "Well, there is one student I'm not sure about, over there in the third row." He pointed with his pointy stick.

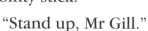

"Stand up, Mr Gill."

The fat fish with a moustache next to W. Rabbit stood up and looked rather embarrassed.

"Is that who you're after? I wouldn't be surprised if he was here by mistake."

Timothy turned to Lyra. "Is that him?" he asked.

"Of course not!" replied Lyra "He's not a rabbit! Rabbit is the one with big ears and a fluffy tail, for goodness sake!"

The fish turned and stared at W. Rabbit. "Are you sure that's him?" said Captain Finn with disbelief. "He's one of our most talented flyers. Maybe you've got the two confused?"

"Tell them, Timothy!" pleaded Lyra. "Tell them he's Rabbit!"

Timothy stood on tiptoes and whispered into Lyra's ear. "Lyra, I've no idea what a rabbit is. Are you sure that's him? I'll believe you if you tell me that's him."

"I've known W. Rabbit all my life, Timothy. Of course I'm sure it's him."

"Captain Finn, we are quite sure, that he is W. Rabbit and he needs to come back with us right away."

"Well, it's quite irregular to have a student leave in the middle of class, but in this case I'll make an exception." Captain Finn turned to W. Rabbit. "It seems that you are in this class under false pretences, Mr Rabbit. However, because you have been such a good student I shall let it pass this time. Good luck in the future and if you ever want to complete your training I'd be happy to see you back."

Finn signaled to the class. "Gentlemen would you please escort Mr Rabbit to the turtle." And they did.

Back inside the turtle ship Lyra couldn't wait. She rushed to the door and flung her arms around Rabbit as soon as he arrived and carried him back inside wrapped in her arms.

"I've got so much to tell you, Rabbit. I've had so many adventures while you were away." She hugged him again. W. Rabbit didn't say anything, but he did look pleased to be back.

Lyra, Timothy and W. Rabbit waved goodbye to the flying fish and the turtle swam away. But they were not heading home. Timothy had another plan that involved a very large octopus.

For the next two days, Lyra, Timothy and W. Rabbit posed for Augustus Tentacle at his studio and, when the portrait was finished, Timothy hung it alongside the paintings of all the other famous turtles in his family.

Timothy was happy to have had an adventure and Lyra was happy too. She sat with W. Rabbit on the rather uncomfortable sofa with the swirly legs, drinking tea from a gold-rimmed cup and listened to Timothy chatting about their adventures. She thought they sounded quite scary and so she hugged W. Rabbit closer and whispered quietly into his ear,

"Don't worry, Rabbit. It's a strange and dangerous world, but you'll be safe as long as you're with me."

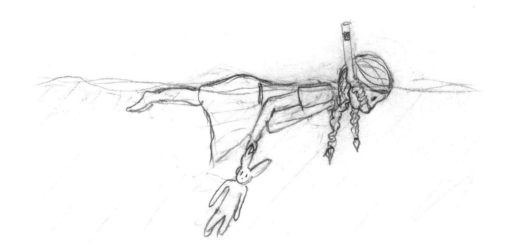

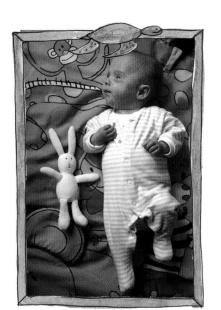

And after her Adventure with the Flying Fish,
Lyra became a bigger person.